W9-AYQ-218

The Little Duckling Who Wouldn't Get Wet

GEK TESSARO

HOLIDAY HOUSE · NEW YORK

DISCARD

RO457521857

The little duckling wouldn't get wet.
No. Not yet.

The big duck patiently explained
that all ducks must swim
and encouraged the little duckling
to jump in the pond.

But the little duckling would NOT get wet.
No. Not yet.

So the big duck tried to PUSH
the little duckling into the water . . .
with no success at all!

The duck called for the cat to help.

The cat pushed the duck
who pushed the duckling
who kept one little webbed foot
firmly on the ground.

So the cat called the dog
who pushed the cat
who pushed the duck
who pushed the duckling
who stood firm.

Then came the turkey
who pushed the dog
who pushed the cat
who pushed the duck
who pushed the duckling
who wouldn't give an inch.

The turkey, the dog, the cat, and the duck
kept pushing and pushing and pushing and pushing.
The duckling was about to topple over
when the turkey screamed,
"A wolf! A wolf!"

And everyone jumped into the pond.
No. Not everyone.

The turkey, the dog, the cat, and the duck shouted, "Jump, duckling! It's the wolf!"

But the duckling didn't think about how wolves eat little birds for snacks. The duckling thought the wolf was one more animal—a big, sharp-toothed, hairy animal—who wanted the duckling to jump in the pond.

And the little duckling wasn't ready to get wet just yet!

The duckling jumped—not into the water, but up in the air—and with all its might, bit the wolf's nose! The wolf ran away in nothing flat!

The turkey, the dog, the cat, and the duck, drenched and embarrassed, left the little duckling at the edge of the pond.

And now the sun is shining and warming the air. The little duckling has made up its mind. It's time to get wet!

Copyright © 2014 by Edizioni lapis
First published in Italian as *Il fatto è* in 2014 by Edizioni lapis, Rome
First published in English in 2020 by Holiday House Publishing, Inc, New York, by arrangement with Atlantyca S.p.A.

English translation © 2020 by Holiday House, Inc.
Translated from the Italian by Grace Maccarone

All Rights Reserved
HOLIDAY HOUSE is registered in the U.S. Patent and Trademark Office.
Printed and bound in January 2020 at Tien Wah Press, Johor Bahru, Johor, Malaysia.
The artwork is cut-paper collage.
www.holidayhouse.com
First Edition
1 3 5 7 9 10 8 6 4 2

Library of Congress Cataloging-in-Publication Data
Names: Tessaro, Gek, author, illustrator. | Maccarone, Grace, translator.
Title: The little duckling who wouldn't get wet / Gek Tessaro ; translated
from the Italian by Grace Maccarone.
Other titles: Fatto è. English | little duckling who wouldn't get wet
Description: New York : Holiday House, 2020. | Originally published in
Italian: Rome : Edizioni lapis, 2014 under the title, Il Fatto è. | Summary:
Despite being pushed by the duck, the cat, the dog, and the turkey, the
little duckling is not ready to get wet, even when a wolf arrives.
Identifiers: LCCN 2019015362 | ISBN 9780823445646 (hardcover)
Subjects: | CYAC: Ducks-Fiction. | Animals-Infancy-Fiction.
Determination (Personality trait)-Fiction. | Animals-Fiction.
Humorous stories. Classification: LCC PZ7.1.T44714 Lit 2020 | DDC [E]-dc23
LC record available at https://lccn.loc.gov/2019015362

No part of this book may be stored, reproduced or transmitted in any form or by any means, electronic or mechanical, including photocopying,
recording or any information storage and retrieval system, without written permission from the copyright holder.